DISCARD

It's Raining!

by Nadia Higgins

illustrated by Damian Ward

Content Consultant: Steven A. Ackerman
Professor of Atmospheric Science
University of Wisconsin-Madison

Weather Watchers

magic Wagon

visit us at www.abdopublishing.com

Published by Magic Wagon, a division of the ABDO Group, 8000 West 78th Street,
Edina, Minnesota 55439. Copyright © 2010 by Abdo Consulting Group, Inc.

Printed in the United States of America, North Mankato, Minnesota.
092009
012010

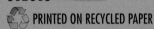 PRINTED ON RECYCLED PAPER

Text by Nadia Higgins
Illustrations by Damian Ward
Edited by Mari Kesselring
Interior layout and design by Nicole Brecke
Cover design by Nicole Brecke

Library of Congress Cataloging-in-Publication Data
Higgins, Nadia.
  It's raining! / by Nadia Higgins ; illustrated by Damian Ward ; content consultant,
Steven A. Ackerman.
        p. cm. — (Weather watchers)
  Includes index.
  ISBN 978-1-60270-733-7
  1. Rain and rainfall—Juvenile literature. I. Ward, Damian, 1977- ill. II. Title.
  QC924.7.H54 2010
  551.57'7—dc22
                                                        2009029378

Table of Contents

Caught in the Rain!

It is a beautiful day. Puffy, white clouds drift by.

Wait a minute. Here comes a tall cloud. *Splat! Splatter! Plop!* It's a rain shower!

Types of Rain

The rain will not last long. Tall, puffy clouds make big drops. But, the rain usually stops as quickly as it started.

What are other types of rain?

Rain always comes from clouds. But not all clouds make rain.

Drizzle is made of small drops. It falls from low, gray clouds. They cover the sky for miles. These clouds can drizzle for days.

Freezing rain is super cold. The raindrops freeze as soon as they hit the ground. Everything's covered in ice. A Freezing Rain Advisory warns people that streets and sidewalks are very slippery.

Thunder booms. Lightning zips. Water pounds the street. Thunderclouds are a type of rain cloud. They are the darkest, tallest clouds.

Inside a thundercloud, tiny bits of ice and water rub against each other. The rubbing causes a giant spark of static electricity. It's lightning!

A water droplet in a cloud is very small. You would need a microscope to see it.

Inside a Cloud

To find out how rain begins, look closely at a cloud. A cloud looks and feels like fog. Clouds are made of millions of tiny water droplets. There can be tiny ice crystals, too.

The tiny drops of water bump into each other. They get bigger. They get too heavy to float. The drops of water fall to Earth as rain.

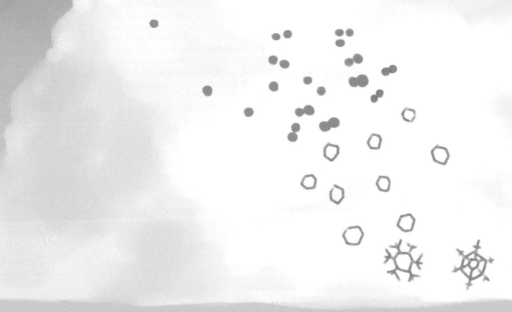

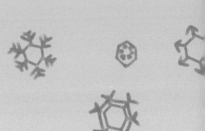

 It's cold high up in the sky. Even in summer, most rain starts as snow.

Rain can also start as ice crystals in the clouds. The ice crystals get too heavy to float. Up high, it snows. But the snowflakes melt on their way down. It's raining!

Tomorrow's Weather

How do we know if it will rain? Scientists study clouds, wind, and temperature. They can get a good idea of what the weather will be. But they cannot tell for sure.

The weather report might give a 90 percent chance of rain. That means rain is probably on the way. The closer the percentage is to 100, the more likely it is that it will rain.

FORECAST

It is often rainy by oceans. Mountain ranges are usually rainy on one side and dry on the other.

Wet Places

In a rain forest, it rains just about every day. Rain forests are in North and South America, Asia, and Africa. These warm, wet forests are filled with many colorful creatures. More than 2,000 kinds of butterflies live in these wet places.

Death Valley, California, is the driest place in North America. The soil is so dry, it's cracked everywhere.

Dry Places

In a desert, it may rain just once a year. The desert animals and plants can live on very little water. For example, a cactus has long roots that grow near the surface of the ground. This way, the roots can slurp up a lot of rain.

Amazing Rain

Rain keeps Earth healthy. It helps plants grow. It fills lakes and rivers that we use for drinking water.

Without rain, there would be no oxygen to breathe. Plants give off oxygen. No rain means no plants. No plants means no oxygen!

When cars, factories, and power plants burn gasoline and oil, they give off harmful gases. The air pollution can get trapped inside clouds. These clouds make acid rain that hurts the planet.

The next time
it rains, maybe you
will be lucky. The sun will
come out while it is raining.
Sunlight streams through the
drops. Can you spot a beautiful
rainbow?

How Rain Forms

1. Tiny water droplets, or ice crystals, bump into each other inside a cloud.

2. The water droplets, or ice crystals, get heavy and fall out of the cloud.

3. Ice crystals melt into water droplets as they fall to Earth.

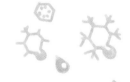

4. The water droplets reach Earth as rain.

Rain Facts

Too Little

Not enough rain causes a drought. During a drought, the soil dries up. Farmers cannot grow crops. Wind blows dry soil away, causing dust storms.

Too Much

If it rains too much, there can be a flood. A flood is when water covers areas that are supposed to be dry, like neighborhoods. Flood-water can damage houses.

The Water Cycle

Rain is part of Earth's amazing recycling program, the water cycle. Earth's water is never lost. It moves from land to sky and back again. As it does, it changes form between liquid, ice, and a gas called water vapor.

Glossary

advisory — a report that tells people what to do in case of bad weather.

air pollution — introducing chemicals and harmful materials into the atmosphere around Earth.

drizzle — light rain that falls in small drops and can last for days.

ice crystals — tiny pieces of ice that can grow into snowflakes.

oxygen — a gas in the air that humans and animals breathe in.

power plant — a factory where electricity is produced.

rain forest — a warm, wet forest.

On the Web

To learn more about rain, visit ABDO Group online at **www.abdopublishing.com**. Web sites about rain are featured on our Book Links page. These links are routinely monitored and updated to provide the most current information available.

Index